D0444120

SECRET SEVEN ON THE TRAIL

SECRET SEVEN ON THE TRAIL

by
ENID BLYTON

Illustrated by
GEORGE BROOK

Hodder
Children's
Books

a division of Hodder Headline

First published in Great Britain in 1952
by Hodder and Stoughton
Revised edition 1992
This millennium edition published 2000

ISBN 0-340-77308-1

Typeset by Hewer Text Ltd, Edinburgh
Printed and bound in Belgium

Hodder Children's Books
a division of Hodder Headline
338 Euston Road
London NW1 3BH

CONTENTS

CHAPTER ONE

The Secret Seven meet

'MUMMY, HAVE you got anything we could have to drink?' asked Janet. 'And to eat too?'

'But you've only *just* finished your breakfast!' said Mummy in surprise. 'And you each had two sausages. You can't possibly want anything more yet.'

'Well, we're having the very last meeting of the Secret Seven this morning,' said Janet. 'Down in the shed. We don't think it's worth while meeting when we all go back to school, nothing exciting ever happens then.'

'We're going to meet again when the Christmas holidays come,' said Peter. 'Aren't we, Scamper, old boy?'

The golden spaniel wagged his tail hard, and gave a small bark.

'He says, he hopes he can come to the last meeting too,' said Janet. 'Of course you can, Scamper.'

'He didn't say that,' said Peter, grinning. 'He said that if there were going to be snacks of any kind at this meeting, he'd like to join in!'

'Woof,' agreed Scamper, and put his paw up on Peter's knee.

'I'll give you lemons, and some sugar, and you can make your own lemonade,' said Mummy. 'You like doing that, don't you? And you can go and see if there are any rock-buns left in the tin in the larder. They'll be stale, but I know you don't mind that!'

'Oh, thanks, Mummy,' said Janet. 'Come on Peter. We'd better get the things now, because the others will be here soon!'

They ran off to the larder, Scamper panting behind. Rock-buns! Stale or not, Scamper liked those as much as the children did.

Janet took some lemons, and went to get the sugar from her mother. Peter emptied the stale rock-buns on to a plate, and the two of them, followed by Scamper, went down to the shed. Janet had the lemon-squeezer and a big jug of water. It was fun to make lemonade.

They pushed open the shed door. On it were the letters S.S. in green – S.S. for the Secret Seven!

'Our Secret Society has been going for some time now,' said Janet, beginning to squeeze a lemon. 'I'm not a bit tired of it, are you, Peter?'

'Of course not!' said Peter. 'Just think of all the adventures we've had, and the exciting things we've done! But I do think it's sensible not to bother about the Secret Seven meetings till the hols. For one thing, in this Christmas term the days get dark very quickly, and we have to be indoors.'

'Yes, and nothing much happens then,' said Janet. 'Oh, Scamper – you won't like that squeezed out lemon-skin, you silly dog! Drop it!'

Scamper dropped it. He certainly didn't like it! He sat with his tongue hanging out, looking most disgusted. Peter glanced at his watch.

'Nearly time for the others to come,' he said. 'I hope they'll agree to this being the last meeting till Christmas. We'd better collect all the badges from them, and put them in a safe place. If we don't, someone is bound to lose one.'

'Or that silly sister of Jack's will take it and wear it herself,' said Janet. 'What's her name – Susie? Aren't you glad I'm not annoying to you, like Susie is to Jack, Peter?'

'Well, you're pretty annoying sometimes,' said Peter, and immediately got a squirt of lemon-juice in his eye from an angry Janet! 'Oh, don't do that. Don't you know that lemon-juice stings like anything? Stop it, Janet!'

Janet stopped it. 'I'd better not waste the juice,' she said. 'Ah, here comes someone.'

Scamper barked as somebody walked up the path and knocked on the door.

'Password!' called Peter, who never opened the door to anyone until the correct password was called.

'Pickled onions!' said a voice, and giggled.

That was the latest password of the Secret Seven, suggested by Colin, whose mother had been pickling onions on the day of the last

4

meeting they had had. It was such a silly password that everyone had laughed, and Peter had said they would have it till they thought of a better one.

'Got your badge?' said Peter, opening the door.

Outside stood Barbara. She displayed her badge proudly. 'It's a new one,' she said. 'My old one's got so dirty, so I made this.'

'Very good,' said Peter. 'Come in. Look, here come three others.'

He shut the door again, and Barbara sat down on a box beside Janet, and watched her stirring the lemonade. Rat-a-tat! Scamper barked as knocking came at the door again.

'Password!' called out Peter, Janet and Barbara together.

'Pickled onions!' yelled back everyone. Peter flung open the door and scowled.

'How MANY times am I to tell you not to yell out the password!' he said. 'Now everyone in hearing distance has heard it.'

'Well, you all yelled out PASSWORD at the tops of your voices,' said Jack. 'Anyway, we can easily choose a new one.' He looked slyly at George, who had come in with him. 'George thought it was pickled cabbage, and we had to tell him it wasn't.'

'Well, of all the – ' began Peter, but just then another knock came on the door and Scamper growled.

'Password!' called Peter.

'Pickled onions!' came his mother's voice, and she laughed. 'If that *is* a password! I've brought you some home-made peppermints, just to help the last meeting along.'

'Oh. Thanks, Mummy,' said Janet, and opened the door. She took the peppermints and gave them to Peter. Peter frowned round, when his mother had gone.

'There you are, you see,' he said. 'It just happened to be my mother who heard the password, but it might have been anybody. Now who's still missing?'

'There's me here, and you, George, Jack, Barbara and Pam,' said Janet. 'Colin's missing. Oh, here he comes.'

Rat-tat! Scamper gave a little welcoming bark. He knew every S.S. member quite well. Colin gave the password and was admitted. Now the Secret Seven were complete.

'Good,' said Peter. 'Sit down, Colin. We'll get down to business as soon as Janet pours out the lemonade. Hurry up, Janet!'

CHAPTER TWO

No more meetings till Christmas!

JANET POURED out mugs of the lemonade, and
Peter handed round the rock-buns.

'A bit stale,' he said, 'but nice and curranty.
Two each and one for old Scamper. Sorry,
Scamper; but, after all, you're not a *real*
member of the Secret Seven, or you could
have two.'

'He couldn't,' said Jack. 'There are only
fifteen buns. And anyway, I *always* count
him in as a real member.'

'You can't. We're the Secret *Seven*, and
Scamper makes eight,' said Peter. 'But he can
always come with us. Now listen, this is to be
the last meeting, and – '

There were surprised cries at once.

'The *last* meeting! Why, what's happening?'

'The *last* one! Surely you're not going to stop the Secret Seven?'

'Oh but, Peter – surely you're not meaning –'

'Just let me *speak*,' said Peter. 'It's to be the last meeting till the holidays come again. Tomorrow all of us boys go back to school, and the girls go to their school the day after. Nothing ever happens in term-time, and anyway we're too busy to look for adventure, so –'

'But something *might* happen,' said Colin. 'You just never know. I think it's a silly idea to stop the Secret Seven for the term-time. I really do.'

'So do I,' said Pam. 'I like belonging to it, and wearing my badge, and remembering the password.'

'Well, you can still wear your badges if you like,' said Peter, 'though I *had* thought of collecting them today, as we're all wearing them, and keeping them till our meeting next hols.'

'I'm not giving *mine* up,' said Jack, firmly. 'And you needn't be afraid I'll let my sister

Susie get it, either, because I've got a perfectly good hiding place for it.'

'And suppose, just *suppose*, something turned up in term-time,' said Colin, earnestly. 'Suppose one of us discovered something strange, something that ought to be looked into. What would we do if the Secret Seven was disbanded till Christmas?'

'Nothing ever turns up in term-time,' repeated Peter, who liked getting his own way. 'And anyway I've got to work hard this term. My

father wasn't at all pleased with my last report.'

'All right. You work hard, and keep out of the Society till Christmas,' said Jack. 'I'll run it with Janet. It can be the Secret Six till then. S.S. will stand for that as much as for Secret Seven.'

That didn't please Peter at all. He frowned. 'No,' he said. 'I'm the head. But seeing that you all seem to disagree with me, I'll say this. We won't have any *regular* meetings, like we have been having, but only call one if anything *does* happen to turn up. And you'll see I'm right.

Nothing will happen!'

'We keep our badges, then, and have a password,' said Colin. 'We're still a very live Society, even if nothing happens. And we'll call a meeting at once if something does?'

'Yes,' said everyone, looking at Peter. They loved being the Secret Seven. It made them feel important, even if, as Colin said, nothing happened for them to look into.

'All right,' said Peter. 'What about a new password?'

Everyone thought hard. Jack looked at Scamper, who seemed to be thinking too. 'What about Scamper's name?' he said. '"Scamper" would be a good password.'

'It wouldn't,' said Janet. 'Every time anyone gave the password Scamper would think he was being called!'

'Let's have *my* dog's name – Rover,' said Pam.

'No, have my aunt's dog's name,' said Jack. 'Cheeky Charlie. That's a good password.'

'Yes! Cheeky Charlie! We'll have that,' said Peter. 'Nobody would ever think of that for a password. Right – Cheeky Charlie it is!'

The rock-buns were passed round for the second time. Scamper eyed them longingly. He had had his. Pam took pity on him and gave him half hers, and Barbara did the same.

Scamper then fixed his eyes mournfully on Jack, who quickly gave him a large piece of his bun too.

'Well!' said Peter. 'Scamper's had more than any real member of the Secret Seven! He'll be thinking he can run the whole Society soon!'

'Wuff,' said Scamper, thumping his tail on the ground, and looking at Peter's bun.

The lemonade was finished. The last crumb of cake had been licked up by Scamper. The sun came out and shone down through the shed window.

'Come on, let's go out and play,' said Peter, getting up. 'School tomorrow! Well, these have been such good hols. Now, Secret Seven, you all know the password, don't you? You probably won't have to use it till the Christmas holidays, so just make up your minds to remember it.'

CHAPTER THREE

The Famous Five

SCHOOL BEGAN for the boys next day, and they all trooped off with their satchels and bags. The girls went off the day after. All the Secret Seven wore their little badges with S.S. embroidered on the button. It was fun to see the other children looking enviously at them, wishing they could have one too.

'No, you can't,' said Janet, when the other girls asked her if they could join. 'It's a *Secret* Society. I'm not supposed even to talk about it.'

'Well, I don't see why you can't make it a bit bigger and let *us* come in,' said the others.

'You can't have more than seven in our Society,' said Janet. 'And we've got seven.

You go and make Secret Societies of your own!'

That was an unfortunate thing to say! Kate and Susie, who was Jack's tiresome sister, immediately went off to make a Society of their own! How very annoying!

They got Harry, Jeff and Sam as well as themselves. Five of them. And then, to the intense annoyance of the Secret Seven, these five appeared at school with badges of their own!

On the buttons they wore were embroidered two letters, not S.S., of course, but F.F. Everyone crowded round to ask what F.F. meant.

'It means "Famous Five",' said Susie. 'We've named ourselves after the Famous Five in the "Five" books! *Much* better idea than "Secret Seven".'

Susie was very irritating to poor Jack. 'You haven't got nearly such a good Society as *we* have,' she said. 'Our badges are bigger, we've got a splendid password, which I wouldn't *dream* of telling you, and we have a secret sign, too. *You* haven't got that!'

'What's your secret sign?' said Jack, crossly. '*I've* never seen you make it.'

16

'Of course not. I tell you it's a *secret* one!' said Susie. 'And we're meeting every single Saturday morning. And, what's more, we've got an adventure going already!'

'I don't believe you,' said Jack. 'Anyway, you're just a copy-cat. It was *our* idea! You're mean.'

'Well, you wouldn't let me belong to your silly Secret Seven,' said Susie, annoyingly. 'Now I belong to the Famous Five, and I tell you, we've got an adventure already!'

17

Jack didn't know whether to believe her or not. He thought Susie must be the most tiresome sister in the world. He wished he had one like Janet. He went gloomily to Peter and told him all that Susie had said.

'Don't take any notice of her,' said Peter. 'Famous Five indeed! They'll soon get tired of meeting and playing about.'

The Famous Five Society was very annoying to the Secret Seven that term. The members wore their big badges every single day. Kate and Susie huddled together in corners at break each morning and talked in excited whispers, as if something really *was* happening.

Harry, Jeff and Sam did the same at their school, which annoyed Peter, Colin, Jack and George very much.

They met in the summer-house in Jack's garden, and Susie actually ordered Jack to keep out of the garden when the 'Famous Five' held their meetings in the summer-house!

'As if I shall keep out of my own garden!' said Jack, indignantly, to Peter. 'But you know Peter, I believe they really *have* got hold of something. I think something *is* up. Wouldn't it be awful if *they* had an adventure and we didn't? Susie would crow like anything.'

Peter thought about this. 'It's up to you to find out about it,' he said, at last. 'After all, they've stolen our idea, and they're doing it to annoy us. You try and find out what's up, Jack. We'll soon put a stop to it!'

So Jack went to hide in a bush at the back of the summer-house when he heard that Susie had planned another meeting there for that Saturday morning. But unfortunately Susie was looking out of the bedroom window just then, and saw him squeezing into the laurel bush!

She gazed down in rage, and then suddenly she smiled. She sped downstairs to meet the other four at the front gate, instead of waiting for them to go down to the summer-house.

They all came together, and Susie began to whisper excitedly.

'Jack's going to try and find out what we're doing! He's hidden himself in the laurel bush at the back of the summer-house to listen to all we say!'

'I'll go and pull him out,' said Harry at once.

'No, don't,' said Susie. 'I've got a better idea. Let's go down to the summer-house, whisper the password so that he can't hear it, and then begin to talk as if we really *had* found an adventure!'

'But why?' said Kate.

'You're silly! Don't you see that Jack will believe it all, and if we mention places such as that old house up on the hill, Tigger's Barn, he'll tell the Secret Seven, and – '

'And they'll all go and investigate it and find there's nothing there!' said Kate, giggling. 'What fun!'

'Yes. And we can mention names too. We'll talk about Stumpy Dick, and – Twisty Tom, and make Jack think we're right in the very middle of something,' said Susie.

'And we could go to Tigger's Barn ourselves and wait till the Secret Seven come, and have a good laugh at them!' said Jeff, grinning. 'Come on, let's go down to the summer-house now, Susie. Jack will be wondering why we are so late.'

'No giggling, anybody!' Susie warned them, 'and just back me up in all I say. And be as solemn as you can. I'll go down first, and you can all come one by one, and don't forget to *whisper* the password, because he mustn't hear *that*.'

She sped down the garden and into the summer-house. Out of the corner of her eye she saw the laurel bush where poor Jack had hidden himself very uncomfortably. Susie grinned to herself. Aha! She was going to have a fine revenge on Jack for keeping her out of *his* Secret Society!

One by one the others came to the summerhouse. They whispered the password, much to Jack's annoyance. He would dearly have loved to pass it on to the Secret Seven! But he couldn't hear a word.

However, he heard plenty when the meeting really began. He couldn't help it, of course, because the Famous Five talked so loudly. Jack didn't guess that it was done on purpose, so that he might hear every word.

He was simply amazed at what the Famous Five said. Why, they seemed to be in the very middle of a Most Exciting Adventure!

CHAPTER FOUR

Susie tells a tale

SUSIE LED the talking. She was a good talker, and was determined to puzzle Jack as much as she could.

'I've found out where those crooks are meeting,' she said. 'It's an important piece of news, so please listen. I've tracked them down at last!'

Jack could hardly believe his ears. He listened hard.

'Tell us, Susie,' said Harry, playing up well.

'It's at Tigger's Barn,' said Susie, enjoying herself. 'That old, deserted house up on the hill. A tumbledown old place, just right for crooks to meet in. Far away from anywhere.'

'Oh yes. I know it,' said Jeff.

'Well, Stumpy Dick and Twisty Tom will both be there,' said Susie.

There were 'oooohs' and 'ahs' from her listeners, and Jack very nearly said 'Ooooh' too. Stumpy Dick and Twisty Tom – good gracious! What *had* the Famous Five got on to?

'They're planning something we must find out about,' said Susie, raising her voice a little, to make sure that Jack could hear. 'And we've simply *got* to do something. So one or two of us must go to Tigger's Barn at the right time and hide ourselves.'

'I'll go with you, Susie,' said Jeff at once.

Jack felt surprised when he heard that. Jeff was a very timid boy, and not at all likely to go and hide in a deserted place like Tigger's Barn. He listened hard.

'All right. You and I will go together,' said Susie. 'It will be dangerous, but what do we care about that? We are the Famous Five!'

'Hurrah!' said Kate and Sam.

'When do we go?' said Jeff.

'Well,' said Susie, 'I *think* they will meet there on Tuesday night. Can you come with me then, Jeff?'

'Certainly,' said Jeff, who would never have *dreamed* of going to Tigger's Barn at night if Susie's tale had been true.

Jack, out in the bush, felt more and more surprised. He also felt a great respect for the Famous Five. My word! They were as good as the Secret Seven! Fancy their getting on to an adventure like this! What a good thing he had managed to hide and hear about it!

He longed to go to Peter and tell him all he

had heard. He wondered how his sister Susie knew anything about this affair. Bother Susie! It was just like her to make a Secret Society and then find an adventure for it.

'Suppose Stumpy Dick discovers you?' said Kate.

'I shall knock him to the ground,' said Jeff in a very valiant voice.

This was going a bit too far. Not even the Famous Five could imagine Jeff facing up to anyone. Kate gave a sudden giggle.

That set Sam off, and he gave one of his extraordinary snorts. Susie frowned. If the meeting began to giggle and snort like this, Jack would certainly know it wasn't serious. That would never do.

She frowned heavily at the others. 'Shut up!' she whispered. 'If we begin to giggle Jack won't believe a word.'

'I c-c-can't help it,' said Kate, who never could stop giggling once she began. 'Oh, Sam, please don't snort again!'

'Sh!' said Susie, angrily. 'Don't spoil it all.' Then she raised her voice again so that Jack could hear. 'Well, Famous Five, that's all for today. Meet again when you get your orders, and remember, don't say a word to ANYONE about Tigger's Barn. This is OUR adventure!'

'I bet the Secret Seven wish they could hear about this,' said Jeff, in a loud voice. 'It makes me laugh to think they don't know anything.'

He laughed, and that was the signal for everyone to let themselves go. Kate giggled again, Sam snorted, Susie roared, and so did Harry. They all thought of Jack out in the laurel bush, drinking in every word of their ridiculous story, and then they laughed all the more. Jack listened crossly. How dare they laugh at the Secret Seven like that?

'Come on,' said Susie, at last. 'This meeting is over. Let's go and get a ball and have a game. I wonder where Jack is? He might like to play too.'

As they all knew quite well where Jack was, this made them laugh again, and they went up the garden path in a very good temper. What a joke to play on a member of the Secret Seven! Would he rush off at once and call a meeting? Would the Secret Seven go to Tigger's Barn on

Tuesday night in the dark?

'Susie, you don't *really* mean to go up to Tigger's Barn on Tuesday night, do you?' said Jeff, as they went up the path.

'Well, I did think of it at first,' said Susie. 'But it would be silly to. It's a long way, and it's dark at night now, and anyway, the Secret Seven might not go, and it would be awfully silly for any of us to go and hide there for nothing!'

'Yes, it would,' said Jeff, much relieved. 'But you'll be able to see if Jack does, won't you, Susie? If he slips off somewhere on Tuesday night, won't we have a laugh!'

'We certainly will!' said Susie. 'Oh, I *do* hope he does! I'll tell him it was all a trick, when he comes back, and won't he be FURIOUS!'

CHAPTER FIVE

Jack tells the news

JACK CREPT carefully out of the laurel bush as soon as he felt sure that the others were safely out of the way. He dusted himself down and looked round. Nobody was in sight.

He debated with himself what to do. Was it important enough to call a meeting of the Secret Seven? No – he would go and find Peter and tell him first. Peter could decide whether to have a meeting or not.

On the way to Peter's house Jack met George. 'Hello!' said George, 'you look very solemn! What's up? Have you had a row at home or something?'

'No,' said Jack. 'But I've just found out that the Famous Five are in the middle of something. I heard Susie telling them, down in our summerhouse. I was in the laurel bush outside.'

'Is it important?' asked George. 'I mean, your sister Susie's a bit of a nuisance, isn't she? You don't want to pay too much attention to her. She's conceited enough already.'

'Yes, I know,' said Jack. 'But she's clever, you know. And after all, *we* managed to get into quite a few adventures, didn't we? And there's really no reason why the Famous Five shouldn't, too, if they keep their eyes and ears open. Listen, and I'll tell you what I heard.'

He told George, and George was most impressed. 'Tigger's Barn!' he said. 'Well, that *would* be a good meeting-place for crooks who wanted to meet without being seen. But how did Susie get hold of the names of the men? Oh Jack, it would be absolutely *maddening* if the Famous Five hit on something important before we did!'

'That's what *I* think,' said Jack. 'Especially as Susie's the ring-leader. She's always trying to boss me, and she would be worse than ever if her silly Society discovered some gang or plot.

Let's find Peter, shall we? I was on the way to him when I met you.'

'I'll go with you, then,' said George. 'I'm sure Peter will think it's important. Come on!'

So two solemn boys walked up the path to Peter's house, and went round the back to find him. He was chopping up firewood, one of his Saturday morning jobs. He was very pleased to see Jack and George.

'Oh, hallo,' he said, putting down his axe. 'Now I can knock off for a bit. Chopping wood is fine for about five minutes, but an awful bore after that. My mother doesn't like me to do it, because she thinks I'll chop my fingers off, but Dad's hard-hearted and makes me do it each Saturday.'

'Peter,' said Jack, 'I've got some news.'

'Oh, what?' asked Peter. 'Tell me.'

So Jack told him about how he had hidden in the laurel bush and overheard a meeting of the Famous Five. 'They've got a password, of course,' he said, 'but I couldn't hear it. However, they forgot to whisper once they had said the password, and I heard every word.'

31

He told Peter what he had heard, but Peter didn't take it seriously. He was most annoying.

He listened to the end, and then he threw back his head and laughed. 'Oh Jack! Surely you didn't fall for all that nonsense? Susie must have been pretending. I expect that's what they do at their silly meetings – pretend they are in the middle of an adventure, and kid themselves they're clever.'

'But it all sounded absolutely serious,' said Jack, beginning to feel annoyed. 'I mean, they had no idea I was listening, they all seemed quite serious. And Jeff was ready to go and investigate on Tuesday evening!'

'What, *Jeff*! Can you imagine that little coward going to look for a *mouse*, let alone Stumpy Dick and the other fellow, whatever his name is!' said Peter, laughing again. 'He'd run a mile before he'd go to Tigger's Barn at night. That sister of yours was just making up a story, Jack, silly kid's stuff, like pretending to play at Red Indians or something, that's all.'

'Then you don't think it's worth while calling a meeting of the Secret Seven and asking some of us to go to Tigger's Barn on Tuesday night?' said Jack, in a hurt voice.

'No, I don't,' said Peter. 'I'm not so stupid as to believe in Susie's fairy-tales.'

'But suppose the Famous Five go, and discover something *we* ought to discover?' said George.

'Well, if Jack sees Susie and Jeff creeping off somewhere on Tuesday evening, he can follow them,' said Peter, still grinning. 'But they won't go! You'll see I'm right. It's all make-believe!'

'All right,' said Jack, getting up. 'If that's what you think there's no use in talking about it any longer. But you'll be sorry if you find you ought to have called a meeting and didn't, Peter! Susie may be a nuisance, but she's jolly clever, *too* clever, and I wouldn't be a bit surprised if the Famous Five weren't beginning an adventure *we* ought to have!'

Peter began to chop wood again, still smiling in a most superior way. Jack marched off, his head in the air, very cross. George went with him. They said nothing for a little while, and then George looked doubtfully at Jack.

'Peter's very certain about it all, isn't he?' he said. 'Do you think he's right? After all, he's

the chief of the Secret Seven. We ought to obey.'

'Look here, George. I'm going to wait and see what Susie does on Tuesday evening,' said Jack. 'If she stays at home, I'll know Peter's right, and it's all make-believe on her part. But if she goes off by herself, or Jeff comes to call for her, I'll know there's something up, and I'll follow them!'

'That's a good idea,' said George. 'I'll come with you, if you like.'

'I don't know what time they'll go, though, if they *do* go,' said Jack. 'I know, you come to tea with me on Tuesday, George. Then we can follow Susie and Jeff at once, if they slip off. And if they don't go out, then we'll know it's nonsense and I'll apologise to Peter the next morning for being so stupid.'

'Right,' said George, pleased. 'I'll come to tea on Tuesday, then, and we'll keep a close watch on Susie. I'm glad I haven't got a sister like that! You never know what she's up to!'

When Jack got home, he went straight to his mother. 'Mother,' he said, 'may I have George to tea on Tuesday, please?'

Susie was there, reading in a corner. She pricked up her ears at once, and grinned in delight. She guessed that Jack and George meant to follow her and Jeff – if they went! All right, she would take the joke a little farther.

'Oh, that reminds me, Mother,' she said. 'Could I have *Jeff* to tea on Tuesday too? It's rather important! I can? Thank you very much!'

CHAPTER SIX

Susie's little trick

JACK WAS pleased when he heard Susie asking for Jeff to come to tea on Tuesday.

'That just proves it!' he said to himself. 'They will slip off to Tigger's Barn together. Peter was quite wrong! Let me see. Tuesday is the evening Mother goes to a Committee Meeting, so Susie and Jeff can go off without anyone bothering. And so can I! Aha! George and I will be on their track all right.'

Jack told George, who agreed that it did look as if there really was something in all that had been said at the meeting of the Famous Five.

'We'll keep a sharp eye on Susie and Jeff, and follow them at once,' said George. 'They'll be most annoyed to find we are with them in Tigger's Barn! We'd better take a torch, Jack. It will be dark.'

'Not awfully dark,' said Jack. 'There will be a moon. But it might be cloudy so we certainly will take a torch.'

Susie told Jeff, with many giggles, that Jack had asked George to tea on Tuesday. 'So I've asked for you to come too,' she said. 'And after tea, Jeff, you and I will slip out secretly, and make Jack and George think we are off to Tigger's Barn, but really and truly we will only be hiding somewhere, and we'll go back and play as soon as we are certain Jack and George have gone off to try and follow us to Tigger's Barn! Oh, dear, they'll go all the way there, and won't find a thing, except a horrid old tumbledown house!'

'It will serve them right!' said Jeff. 'All I can say is that I'm very glad *I'm* not going off to that lonely place at night.'

Tuesday afternoon came, and with it came Jeff and George after school, on their way to tea with Jack and Susie. The two boys walked with Jack, who pretended to be astonished that Jeff should go to tea with Susie.

'Going to play with her dolls?' he asked. 'Or perhaps you're going to spring-clean the dolls' house?'

Jeff went red. 'Don't be stupid,' he said. 'I've got my new railway set with me. We're going to play with that.'

'But it takes ages to set out on the floor,' said Jack, surprised.

'Well, what of it?' said Jeff, scowling. Then he remembered that Jack and George thought that he and Susie were going off to Tigger's Barn, and would naturally imagine that he wouldn't have time to play such a lengthy game as trains. He grinned to himself. Let Jack be puzzled! It would do him good!

They all had a very good tea, and then went to the playroom upstairs. Jeff began to set out his railway lines. Jack and George would have liked to help, but they were afraid that Susie might point out that Jeff was *her* guest, not theirs. Susie had a very sharp tongue when she liked!

So they contented themselves with trying to

make a rather complicated model aeroplane, keeping a sharp eye on Susie and Jeff all the time.

Very soon Jack's mother put her head in at the door. 'Well, I'm off to my Committee Meeting,' she said. 'You must both go home at eight o'clock, Jeff and George – and Jack, if I'm not back in time for your supper, make yourselves something, and then go and have your baths.'

'Right, Mother,' said Jack. 'Come and say good-night to us when you get back.'

As soon as her mother had gone, Susie went all mysterious. She winked at Jeff, who winked back. Jack saw the winks, of course. They meant him to! He was on the alert at once. Ah, those two were probably going to slip out into the night!

'Jeff, come and see the new clock we've got downstairs,' said Susie. 'It has a little man who comes out at the top and strikes a hammer on an anvil to mark every quarter of an hour. It is nearly a quarter past seven, let's go and watch him come out.'

'Right,' said Jeff, and the two went out, nudging each other, and laughing.

'There they go,' said George. 'Do we follow them straightaway?'

Jack went to the door. 'They've gone downstairs,' he said. 'They will get their coats out of the hall cupboard. We'll give them a minute to put them on, then we'll get ours. We shall hear the front door bang, I expect. It won't take us a minute to follow them.'

In about a minute they heard the front door being opened, and then it shut rather quietly, as if it was not really meant to be heard.

'Did you hear that?' asked Jack. 'They shut it very quietly. Come on, we'll pull on our coats and follow. We don't want to track them too closely, or they'll see us. We will certainly surprise them when they get to Tigger's Barn, though!'

They put on their coats, and opened the front door. It was fairly light outside because of the rising moon. They took a torch with them, in case the clouds became thick.

There was no sign of Jeff and Susie.

'They have gone at top speed, I should think!' said Jack, closing the door behind him. 'Come on, we know the way to Tigger's Barn, even if we don't spot Jeff and Susie in front of us.'

They went down the garden path. They did not hear the giggles that followed them! Jeff and Susie were hiding behind the big hall curtains, and were now watching Jack and George going down the path. They clutched one another as they laughed. What a fine joke they had played on the two boys!

CHAPTER SEVEN

At Tigger's Barn

JACK AND GEORGE had no idea at all that they
had left Jeff and Susie behind them in the hall.
They imagined that the two were well in front
of them, hurrying to Tigger's Barn! They
hurried too, but, rather to their surprise, they
did not see any children in front, however
much they strained their eyes in the moonlit
night.

'Well, all I can say is they must have taken
bicycles,' said George, at last. 'They *couldn't*
have gone so quickly. Has Susie a bike, Jack?'

'Oh yes, and I bet she's lent Jeff mine,' said
Jack, crossly. 'They'll be at Tigger's Barn ages
before us. I hope the meeting of those men isn't
over before we get there. I don't want Susie and

Jeff to hear everything without us hearing it too!'

Tigger's Barn was about a mile away. It was up on a lonely hill, hemmed in by trees. Once it had been part of a farmhouse, which had been burnt down one night. Tigger's Barn was now only a tumbledown shell of a house, used by tramps who needed shelter, by jackdaws who nested in the one remaining enormous chimney, and by a big tawny owl who used it to sleep in during the daytime.

Children had played in it until they had been forbidden to in case the old walls gave way. Jack and George had once explored it with Peter, but an old tramp had risen up from a corner and shouted at them so loudly that they had fled away.

The two boys trudged on. They came to the hill and walked up the narrow lane that led to Tigger's Barn. Still there was no sign of Jeff or Susie. Well, if they had taken bicycles, they would certainly be at Tigger's Barn by now!

They came to the old building at last. It stood there in the rather dim moonlight, looking forlorn and bony, with part of its roof missing, and its one great chimney sticking up into the night sky.

'Here we are,' whispered Jack. 'Walk quietly, because we don't want to let Jeff and Susie know we're here, or those men either, if they've come already! But everything is very quiet. I don't think the men are here.'

They kept in the shadow of a great yew hedge, and made their way on tiptoe to the back of the house. There was a front door and a back door, and both were locked, but as no window had glass in, it was easy enough for anyone to get inside the tumbledown place if they wanted to.

Jack clambered in through a downstairs window. A scuttling noise startled him, and he clutched George and made him jump.

'Don't grab me like that,' complained George, in a whisper. 'It was only a rat hurrying away. You nearly made me yell when you grabbed me so suddenly.'

'Sh!' said Jack. 'What's that?'

They listened. Something was moving high up in the great chimney that towered from the hearth in the broken-down room they were in.

'Maybe it's the owl,' said George, at last. 'Yes, listen to it hooting.'

A quavering hoot came to their ears. But it didn't really sound as if it came from the chimney. It seemed to come from outside the house, in the overgrown garden. Then an answering hoot came, but it didn't sound at all like an owl.

'Jack,' whispered George, his mouth close to Jack's ear, 'that's not an owl. It's men signalling to one another. They *are* meeting here! But where are Susie and Jeff?'

'I don't know. Hidden safely somewhere, I expect,' said Jack, suddenly feeling a bit shaky at the knees. 'We'd better hide too. Those men will be here in half a minute.'

'There's a good hiding-place over there in the hearth,' whispered George. 'We can stand there in the darkness, right under the big chimney. Come on, quick. I'm sure I can hear footsteps outside.'

The two boys ran silently to the hearth. Tramps had made fires there from time to time, and a heap of ashes half-filled the hearth. The boys stood ankle-deep in them, hardly daring to breathe.

Then a torch suddenly shone out, and raked the room with its beam. Jack and George pressed close together, hoping they did not show in the great hearth.

They heard the sound of someone climbing in through the same window they had come in by. Then a voice spoke to someone outside.

'Come on in. Nobody's here. Larry hasn't come yet. Give him the signal, Zeb, in case he's waiting about for it now.'

Somebody gave a quavering hoot again. 'Ooooo-oo-oo! Ooooo, ooo-oo-oo!'

An answering call came from some way away, and after about half a minute another man climbed in. Now there were three.

The two boys held their breath. Good gracious! They were right in the middle of something very strange! Why were these men meeting at this tumbledown place? Who were they and what were they doing?

Where were Susie and Jeff, too? Were they listening and watching as well?

'Come into the next room,' said the man who had first spoken. 'There are boxes there to sit on, and a light won't shine out there as much as it does from this room. Come on, Larry – here, Zeb, shine your torch in front.'

CHAPTER EIGHT

An uncomfortable time

THE TWO boys were half-glad, half-sorry that the men had gone into another room. Glad because they were no longer afraid of being found, but sorry because it was now impossible to hear clearly what the men were saying.

They could hear a murmur from the next room.

Jack nudged George. 'I'm going to creep across the floor and go to the door. Perhaps I can hear what they are saying then,' he whispered.

'No, don't,' said George, in alarm. 'We'll be discovered. You're sure to make a noise!'

'I've got rubber-soled shoes on. I shan't make a sound,' whispered back Jack. 'You stay here, George. I DO wonder where Susie and Jeff are. I hope I don't bump into them anywhere.'

Jack made his way very quietly to the doorway that led to the next room. There was a broken door still hanging there, and he could peep through the crack. He saw the three men in the room beyond, sitting on old boxes, intently studying a map of some kind, and talking in low voices.

If only he could hear what they said! He tried to see what the men were like, but it was too dark. He could only hear their voices, one a polished voice speaking clearly and firmly, and the other two rough and unpleasant.

Jack hadn't the slightest idea what they were talking about. Loading and unloading. Six-two or maybe seven-ten. Points, points, points. There mustn't be a moon. Darkness, fog, mist. Points. Fog. Six-two, but it might go as long as seven-twenty. And again, points points, points.

What in the world could they be discussing? It was maddening to hear odd words like this that made no sense. Jack strained his ears to try and make out more, but it was no use, he couldn't. He decided to edge a little nearer.

He leaned against something that gave way behind him. It was a cupboard door! Before he could stop himself Jack fell inside, landing with a soft thud. The door closed on him with a little click. He sat there, alarmed and astonished, not daring to move.

'What was that?' said one of the men.

They all listened, and at that moment a big rat ran silently round the room, keeping to the wall. One of the men picked it out in the light of his torch.

'Rats,' he said. 'This place is alive with them. That's what we heard.'

'I'm not sure,' said the man with the clear voice. 'Switch off that light, Zeb. Sit quietly for a bit and listen.'

The light was switched off. The men sat in utter silence, listening. Another rat scuttered over the floor.

Jack sat absolutely still in the cupboard, fearful that the men might come to find out who had made a noise. George stood in the hearth of the next room, wondering what had happened. There was such dead silence now, and darkness too!

The owl awoke in the chimney above him, and stirred once more. Night-time! It must go hunting. It gave one soft hoot and dropped down the chimney to make its way out through the bare window.

It was as startled to find George standing at the bottom of the chimney as George was startled to feel the owl brushing his cheek. It flew silently out of the window, a big moving shadow in the dimness.

George couldn't bear it. He must get out of this chimneyplace, he must! Something else might fall down on him and touch his face softly. Where was Jack? How mean of him to go off and leave him with things that lived in chimneys! And Jack had the torch with him too. George would have given anything to flick on the light of a torch.

He crept out of the hearth, and stood in the middle of the floor, wondering what to do. What *was* Jack doing? He had said he was going to the doorway that led to the next room, to see if he could hear what the men said. But were the men there now? There wasn't a sound to be heard.

Perhaps they have slipped out of another window and gone, thought poor George. If so why doesn't Jack come back? It's horrid of him. I can't bear this much longer.

He moved over to the doorway, putting out his hands to feel if Jack was there. No, he wasn't. The next room was in black darkness, and he couldn't see a thing there. There was also complete silence. Where *was* everyone?

George felt his legs giving way at the knees. This horrible old tumbledown place! Why ever had he listened to Jack and come here with him? He was sure that Jeff and Susie hadn't been stupid enough to come here at night.

He didn't dare to call out. Perhaps Jack was somewhere nearby, scared too. What about the Secret Seven password? What was it now? Cheeky Charlie!

If I whisper Cheeky Charlie, Jack will know it's me, he thought. It's our password. He'll know it's me, and he'll answer.

So he stood at the doorway and whispered: 'Cheeky Charlie! Cheeky Charlie!'

No answer. He tried again, a little louder this time, 'Cheeky Charlie!'

And then a torch snapped on, and caught him directly in its beam. A voice spoke to him harshly.

'What's all this? What do you know about Charlie? Come right into the room, boy, and answer my question.'

CHAPTER NINE

Very peculiar

GEORGE WAS extremely astonished. Why, the men were still there! Then where was Jack? What had happened to him? He stood there in the beam of the torch, gaping.

'Come on in,' said the voice, impatiently. 'We heard you saying "Cheeky Charlie". Have you got a message from him?'

George gaped still more. A message from him? From Cheeky Charlie? Why, that was only a password! Just the name of a dog! What did the man mean?

'*Will* you come into the room?' said the man, again. 'What's the matter with you, boy? Are you scared? We shan't eat a messenger from Charlie.'

George went slowly into the room, his mind suddenly working at top speed. A messenger from Charlie. Could there be someone called Charlie, Cheeky Charlie? Did these men think he had come from him? How very extra-ordinary!

'There won't be no message from Charlie,' said the man called Zeb. 'Why should there be? He's waiting for news from *us*, isn't he? Here, boy – did Charlie send you to ask for news?'

George could do nothing but nod his head. He didn't want to have to explain anything at all. These men appeared to think he had come to find them to get news for someone called Charlie. Perhaps if he let them give him the message, they would let him go without any further questions.

'Can't think why Charlie uses such a dumb kid to send out,' grumbled Zeb. 'Got a pencil, Larry? I'll scribble a message.'

'A kid that can't open his mouth and speak a word is just the right messenger for us,' said the man with the clear voice. 'Tell Charlie what we've decided, Zeb. Don't forget that he's to

mark the tarpaulin with white lines at one corner.'

Zeb scribbled something in a note-book by the light of a torch. He tore out the page and folded it over. 'Here you are,' he said to George. 'Take this to Charlie, and don't you go calling him Cheeky Charlie, see? Little boys that are rude get their ears boxed! His friends can call him what they like, but not you.'

'Oh, leave the kid alone,' said Larry. 'Where's Charlie now, kid? At Dalling's or at Hammond's?'

George didn't know what to answer. 'Dalling's,' he said at last, not knowing in the least what it meant.

Larry tossed him fifty pence. 'Clear off!' he said. 'You're scared stiff of this place, aren't you? Want me to take you down the hill?'

This was the last thing that poor George wanted. He shook his head.

The men got up. 'Well, if you want company, we're all going now. If not, buzz off.'

George buzzed off, but not very far. He went back again into the other room, thankful to see that the moon had come out again, and had lit it enough for him to make his way quickly to the window. He clambered out awkwardly, because his legs were shaking and were not easy to manage.

He made for a thick bush and flung himself into the middle. If those men really were going, he could wait till they were gone. Then he could go back and find Jack. WHAT had happened to Jack? He seemed to have disappeared completely.

The men went cautiously out of Tigger's Barn, keeping their voices low. The owl flew over their heads, giving a sudden hoot that startled them. Then George heard them laugh. Their footsteps went quietly down the hill.

He heaved a sigh of relief. Then he scrambled out of the bush and went back into the house. He stood debating what to do. Should he try the password again? It had had surprising results last time, so perhaps this time it would be better just to call Jack's name.

But before he could do so, a voice came out of the doorway that led to the further room.

'Cheeky Charlie!' it said, in a piercing whisper.

George stood stock still, and didn't answer. Was it Jack saying that password? Or was it somebody else who knew the real Cheeky Charlie, whoever he might be?

Then a light flashed on and caught him in its beam. But this time, thank goodness, it was Jack's torch, and Jack himself gave an exclamation of relief.

'It *is* you, George! Why in the world didn't

you answer when I said the password? You must have known it was me.'

'Oh, Jack! Where were you? I've had an awful time!' said George. 'You shouldn't have gone off and left me like that. Where have you been?'

'I was listening to those men, and fell into this cupboard,' said Jack. 'It shut on me, and I couldn't hear another word. I didn't dare to move in case those men came to look for me. But at last I opened the door, and when I couldn't hear anything, I wondered where *you* were! So I whispered the password.'

'Oh, I see,' said George, thankfully. 'So you didn't hear what happened to *me*? The men discovered me – and – '

'*Discovered* you! What did they do?' said Jack, in the greatest astonishment.

'It's really very peculiar,' said George. 'You see, *I* whispered the password too, hoping *you* would hear it. But the *men* heard me whispering "Cheeky Charlie", and they called me in and asked me if I was a messenger from him.'

Jack didn't follow this, and it took George a

little time to explain to him that the three men seemed really to think that someone they knew, who actually *was* called Cheeky Charlie, was using George as a messenger!

'And they gave *me* a message for him,' said George. 'In a note. I've got it in my pocket.'

'No! Have you really!' said Jack, suddenly excited. 'Gosh, this is thrilling. We might be in the middle of an adventure again. Let's see the note.'

'No. Let's go home and then read it,' said George. 'I want to get out of this tumbledown old place, I don't like it a bit. Something came down the chimney on me, and I nearly had a fit. Come on, Jack, I want to go.'

'Yes, but wait,' said Jack, suddenly remembering. 'What about Susie and Jeff? They must be somewhere here too. We ought to look for them.'

'We'll have to find out how they knew there was to be a meeting here tonight,' said George. 'Let's call them, Jack. Honestly, there's nobody else here now. *I'm* going to call them anyway!'

So he shouted loudly: 'JEFF! SUSIE! COME ON OUT, WHEREVER YOU ARE!'

His voice echoed through the old house, but nobody stirred, nobody answered.

'I'll go through the place with the torch,' said Jack, and the two boys went bravely into each broken-down, bare room, flashing the light all round.

There was no one to be seen. Jack suddenly felt anxious. Susie was his sister. What had happened to her?

'George, we must go back home as quickly as we can, and tell Mother that Susie's disappeared,' he said. 'And Jeff has too. Come on quick! Something may have happened to them.'

They went back to Jack's house as quickly as they could. As they ran to the front gate, Jack saw his mother coming back from her meeting. He rushed to her.

'Mother! Susie's missing! She's gone! Oh, Mother, she went to Tigger's Barn, and now she isn't there!'

His mother looked at him in alarm. She opened the front door quickly and went in, followed by the two boys.

'Now tell me quickly,' she said. 'What do you mean? Why did Susie go out? When – '

A door was flung open upstairs and a merry voice called out: 'Hallo, Mother! Is that you? Come and see Jeff's railway going! And don't scold us because it's so late; we've been waiting for Jack and George to come back.'

'Why, that's Susie,' said her mother, in surprise. 'What did you mean, Jack, about Susie disappearing. What a silly joke!'

Sure enough, there were Susie and Jeff

upstairs, with the whole floor laid out with railway lines!

Jack stared at Susie in surprise and indignation. Hadn't she gone out, then? She grinned at him wickedly.

'Serves you right!' she said rudely. 'Who came spying on our Famous Five meeting? Who heard all sorts of things and believed them? Who's been all the way to Tigger's Barn in the dark? Who's a silly-billy, who's a – '

Jack rushed at her in a rage. She dodged behind her mother, laughing.

'Now, Jack, now!' said his mother. 'Stop that, please. What has been happening? Susie, go to bed. Jeff, clear up your lines. It's time for you to go. Your mother will be telephoning to ask why you are not home. JACK! Did you hear what I said? Leave Susie alone.'

Jeff went to take up his lines, and George helped him. Both boys were scared of Jack's mother when she was cross. Susie ran to her room and slammed the door.

'She's a wicked girl,' raged Jack, 'she – she – she – '

'Go and turn on the bath-water,' said his

mother, sharply. 'You can both go without your supper now. I WILL NOT have this behaviour.'

George and Jeff disappeared out of the house as quickly as they could, carrying the boxes of railway things. George completely forgot what he had in his pocket – a pencilled note to someone called Cheeky Charlie, which he hadn't even read! Well, well, well!

CHAPTER TEN

Call a meeting!

GEORGE WENT quickly along the road with Jeff. Jeff chuckled.

'I say, you and Jack fell for our little trick beautifully, didn't you? Susie's clever, she laid her plan well. We all talked at the tops of our voices so that Jack would be sure to hear. We knew he was hiding in the laurel bush.'

George said nothing. He was angry that Susie and the Famous Five should have played a trick like that on the Secret Seven – angry that Jack had been so easily taken in – but, dear me, what curious results that trick had had!

Susie had mentioned Tigger's Barn just to make Jack and the Secret Seven think that the

Famous Five had got hold of something that was going on there, and had talked about a make-believe Stumpy Dick and Twisty Tom. And lo and behold, something *was* going on there, not between Stumpy Dick and Twisty Tom, but between three mysterious fellows called Zeb, Larry, and had he heard the other man's name? No, he hadn't.

'You're quiet, George,' said Jeff, chuckling again. 'How did you enjoy your visit to Tigger's Barn? I bet it was a bit frightening!'

'It was,' said George, truthfully, and said no more. He wanted to think about everything carefully, to sort out all he had heard, to try and piece together what had happened. It was all jumbled up in his mind.

One thing's certain, he thought, suddenly. We'll have to call a meeting of the Secret Seven. How strange that the Famous Five should have played a silly joke on us and led us to Something Big – another adventure, I'm sure. Susie's an idiot, but she's done the Secret Seven a very good turn!

As soon as George got home he felt in his pocket for the note that Zeb had given him. He felt round anxiously. It would have been dreadful if he had lost it!

But he hadn't. His fingers closed over the folded piece of paper. He took it out, his hand trembling with excitement. He opened it, and read it by the light of his bedroom lamp.

Dear Charlie,

Everything's ready and going O.K. Can't see that anything can go wrong, but a fog would be very welcome as you can guess! Larry's looking after the points, we've arranged that. Don't forget the lorry, and get the tarpaulin truck cover marked with white at one corner. That'll save time in looking for the right load. It's clever of you to send out this load by truck, and collect it by lorry!

All the best,
Zeb

George couldn't make head or tail of this. What in the world was it all about? There was a plot of some kind, that was clear, but what did everything else mean?

CALL A MEETING!

George went to the telephone. Perhaps Peter wouldn't yet be in bed. He really MUST get on to him and tell him something important had happened.

Peter was just going to bed. He came to the telephone in surprise, when his mother called him to it.

'Hallo! What's up?'

'Peter, I can't stop to tell you everything now, but we went to Tigger's Barn, Jack and I, and there *is* something going on. We had quite an adventure, and – '

'You don't mean to tell me that that tale of Susie's was true!' said Peter, disbelievingly.

'No. At least, it was all made-up on her part, as you said, but all the same, something *is* going on at Tigger's Barn, Peter, something Susie didn't know about, of course, because she only mentioned the place in fun. But it's serious, Peter. You must call a meeting of the Secret Seven tomorrow evening after tea.'

There was a pause.

'Right,' said Peter, at last. 'I will. This is most odd, George. Don't tell me anything more over the phone, because I don't want Mother asking me too many questions. I'll tell Janet to tell Pam and Barbara there's a meeting tomorrow evening at five o'clock in our shed, and we'll tell Colin and Jack. Gosh! This sounds pretty mysterious.'

'You just wait till you hear the whole story!' said George. 'You'll be amazed.'

He put down the receiver, and got ready for bed, quite forgetting that he had had no supper. He couldn't stop thinking about the happenings of the evening. How odd that the password of the Secret Seven should be Cheeky Charlie, and there should be a real man called by that name!

And how extraordinary that Susie's bit of make-believe should suddenly have come true without her knowing it! Something *was* going on at Tigger's Barn!

He got into bed and lay awake for a long time. Jack was also lying awake thinking. He was excited. He wished he hadn't been shut up in that silly cupboard, when he might have been listening all the time. Still, George seemed to have got quite a lot of information.

The Secret Seven were very thrilled the next day. It was difficult not to let the Famous Five see that they had something exciting on hand, but Peter had strictly forbidden anyone to talk about the matter at school, just in *case* that tiresome Susie, with her long ears, got to hear of it.

'We don't want the Famous Five trailing us

around,' said Peter. 'Just wait till this evening, all of you, and then we'll really get going!'

At five o'clock every single member of the Secret Seven was in the shed in Peter's garden. All of them had raced home quickly after afternoon school, gobbled their teas, and come rushing to the meeting.

The password was whispered quickly, as one after another passed into the shed, each wearing the badge with S.S. on. 'Cheeky Charlie, Cheeky Charlie, Cheeky Charlie.'

Jack and George had had little time to exchange more than a few words with one another. They were bursting to tell their strange story!

'Now, we're all here,' said Peter. 'Scamper, sit by the door and keep guard. Bark if you hear anything at all. This is a most important meeting.'

Scamper got up and went solemnly to the door. He sat down by it, listening, looking very serious.

'Oh, do hurry up, Peter,' said Pam. 'I can't wait a minute more to hear what it's all about!'

'All right, all right,' said Peter. 'You know

that we weren't going to call another meeting till the Christmas hols, unless something urgent happened. Well, it's happened. Jack, you start off with the story, please.'

Jack was only too ready to tell it. He described how he had hidden in the laurel bush to overhear what the Famous Five said at their meeting in the summer-house. He repeated the ridiculous story that Susie had invented to deceive the Secret Seven, and to send them off on a wild-goose chase just to make fun of them.

He told them how Peter had laughed at the story and said it *was* just in Susie's imagination, but how he and George had decided to go to Tigger's Barn just in case it wasn't.

'But I was right,' interrupted Peter. 'It *was* a story, but just by chance there was some truth in it, too, though Susie didn't know.'

George took up the tale. He told the others how he and Jack had gone to Tigger's Barn, thinking that Susie and Jeff were in front of them. And then came the thrilling part of their adventure in the old tumbledown house!

Everyone listened intently, and held their

breath when George came to the bit where the three men arrived.

Then Jack told how he went to the doorway to listen, and fell into the cupboard, and George told how he had gone to look for Jack, and had said the password, Cheeky Charlie, which had had such surprising results.

'Do you mean to say, there actually *is* a man called Cheeky Charlie?' asked Barbara, in

amazement. 'Our password is only the name of a dog. Imagine there being a *man* called that, too! My goodness!'

'Don't interrupt,' said Peter. 'Go on, both of you.'

Everyone sat up with wide eyes when George told how the men had thought he was a messenger from Cheeky Charlie, and when he told them about the note they had given

him, and produced it from his pocket, the Secret Seven were speechless with excitement!

The note was passed from hand to hand. Peter rapped on a box at last.

'We've all seen the note now,' he said. 'And we've heard Jack and George tell what happened last night. It's quite clear that we've hit on something strange again. Do the Secret Seven think we should try and solve this new mystery?'

Everyone yelled and banged on boxes, and Scamper barked in excitement too.

'Right,' said Peter. 'I agree too. But we have got to be very, very careful this time, or else the Famous Five will try and interfere, and they might spoil everything. Nobody – NOBODY – must say a single word about this to anyone in the world. Is that agreed?'

It was. Scamper came up and laid a big paw on Peter's knee, as if he thoroughly agreed too.

'Go back to the door, Scamper,' said Peter. 'We depend on you to give us warning if any of those tiresome Famous Five come snooping round. On guard, Scamper.'

Scamper trotted back to his place by the door obediently. The Seven crowded more closely together, and began a grand discussion.

'First, let's sort out all the things that Jack and George heard,' said Peter. 'Then we'll try and make out what they mean. At the moment I'm in a muddle about everything and haven't the slightest idea what the men are going to do.'

'Right,' said Jack. 'Well, as I told you, I heard the men talking, but their voices were very low, and I could only catch words now and again.'

'What words were they?' asked Peter. 'Tell us carefully.'

'Well, they kept saying something about "loading and unloading",' said Jack. 'And they kept on and on mentioning "points".'

'What sort of points?' asked Peter.

Jack shook his head, completely at a loss.

'I've no idea. They mentioned figures too. They said "six-two" quite a lot of times, and then they said "maybe seven-ten". And they said there mustn't be a moon, and I heard them talk about darkness, fog, and mist. Honestly, I couldn't make head or tail of it. I only know they must have been discussing some plan.'

'What else did you hear?' asked Janet.

'Nothing,' answered Jack. 'I fell into the cupboard then, and when the door shut on me I couldn't hear another word.'

'And all *I* can add is that the men asked me if Cheeky Charlie was at Dalling's or Hammond's,' said George. 'But goodness knows what *that* meant.'

'Perhaps they are the name of a workshop or works of some kind,' suggested Colin. 'We could find out.'

'Yes. We might be able to trace those,' said Peter. 'Now, this note. Whatever can it mean? It's got the word "points" here again. And they talk about trucks and lorries. It's plain that there's some robbery planned, I think. But what kind? They want fog, too. Well, that's understandable, I suppose.'

'Shall we take the note to the police?' said Barbara, suddenly gripped by a bright idea.

'Oh no! Not yet!' said George. 'It's *my* note and I'd like to see if we can't do something about it ourselves before we tell any grownups. After all, we've managed lots of adventures very well so far. I don't see why we shouldn't be able to do something about this one too.'

'I'm all for trying,' said Peter. 'It's so exciting. And we've got quite a lot to go on, really. We know the names of three of the four men – Zeb, which is probably short for Zebedee, a most unusual name; and Larry, probably short for Laurence; and Cheeky Charlie, who is perhaps the boss.'

'Yes, and we know he's at Dalling's or Hammond's,' said Jack. 'What do we do first, Peter?'

Scamper suddenly began to bark wildly and scrape at the door.

'Not another word!' said Peter, sharply. 'There's someone outside!'

CHAPTER ELEVEN

Any ideas?

PETER OPENED the door. Scamper tore out, barking. Then he stopped by a bush and wagged his tail. The Secret Seven ran to him.

A pair of feet showed at the bottom of the bush. Jack gave a shout of rage and pushed into the bush. He dragged someone out – Susie!

'How dare you!' he yelled. 'Coming here and listening! How dare you, Susie?'

'Let me go,' said Susie. 'I like you asking me how I dare! I'm only copying what *you* did on Saturday! Who hid in the laurel bush, and – '

'How did you know we were having a meeting?' demanded Jack, shaking Susie.

'I just followed you,' said Susie, grinning. 'But I didn't hear anything because I didn't dare to go near the door, in case Scamper barked. I did a sudden sneeze, though, and he must have heard me. What are you calling a meeting about?'

'As if we'd tell you!' said Peter, crossly. 'Go on home, Susie. Go on! Jack, take her home. The meeting is over.'

'Bother!' said Jack. 'All right. Come on, Susie. And if I have any nonsense from you, I'll pull your hair till you yell!'

Jack went off with Susie. Peter faced round to the others and spoke in a low voice.

'Listen. All of you think hard about what has been said, and give me or Janet any good ideas tomorrow. It's no good going on with this meeting. Somebody else belonging to the Famous Five might come snooping round too.'

'Right,' said the Secret Seven, and went home, excited and very much puzzled. *How* could they think of anything that would help to piece together the jumble of words they knew? Points. Six-two, seven-ten. Fog, mist, darkness. Dalling's. Hammond's.

Each of them tried to think of some good idea. Barbara could think of nothing at all.

Pam tried asking her father about Dalling's or Hammond's. He didn't know either of them. Pam felt awkward when he asked her why she wanted to know, and didn't go on with the subject.

Colin decided that a robbery was going to be done one dark and foggy night, and that the goods were to be unloaded from a lorry somewhere. He couldn't imagine why they were to be sent in a truck. All the boys thought exactly the same thing, but, as Peter said, it wasn't much help because they didn't know what date, what place, or what lorry!

Then Jack had quite a good idea. He thought it would be helpful if they tried to find a man called Zebedee, because surely he must be the Zeb at Tigger's Barn. There couldn't be *many* Zebedees in the district!

'All right, Jack. It's a good *idea*,' said Peter. 'You can do the finding out for us. Produce this Zeb, and that may be the first step.'

'Yes, but how shall I find out?' said Jack. 'I can't go round asking every man I meet if he's called Zeb.'

'No. That's why I said it was a good *idea*,'

said Peter, grinning. 'But that's about all it is. It's an impossible thing to do, you see; so that's why it will remain just a good idea and nothing else. Finding the only Zebedee in the district would be like looking for a needle in a hay-stack.'

'I shouldn't like to have to do *that*,' said Janet, who was with them. 'Peter and I have got about the only good idea, I think, Jack.'

'What's that?' asked Jack.

'Well, we looked in our telephone directory at home to see if any firm called Dalling or Hammond was there,' said Janet. 'But there wasn't, so we thought they must be somewhere farther off, not in our district at all. Our telephone book only gives the names of people in this area, you see.'

'And now we're going to the post-office to look in the big telephone directories there,' said Peter. 'They give the names of districts much farther away. Like to come with us?'

Jack went with them. They came to the post-office and went in. Peter took up two telephone books, one with the Ds in and one with the Hs.

'Now I'll look for Dalling,' he said, and

thumbed through the Ds. The other two leaned over him, looking down the Ds too.

'Dale, Dale, Dale, Dales, Dalgleish, Daling, Dalish, Dallas, DALLING!' read Peter, his finger following down the list of names. 'Here it is – Dalling. Oh, there are three Dallings! Bother!'

'There's a Mrs A. Dalling, Rose Cottage, Hubley,' said Janet. 'And E.A. Dalling, of Manor House, Tallington, and Messrs. E. Dalling, Manufacturers of Lead Goods. Well – which would be the right Dalling? The manufacturers, I suppose.'

'Yes,' said Peter, sounding excited. 'Now for the Hs. Where are they? In the other book. Here we are – Hall, Hall – goodness, what a lot of people are called Hall! Hallet, Ham, Hamm, Hammers, Hamming, Hammond, Hammond, Hammond, Hammond – oh, LOOK!'

They all looked. Peter was pointing to the fourth name of Hammond. 'Hammond and Co.' Ltd. Lead manufacturers, Petlington.'

'There you are,' said Peter, triumphantly. 'Two firms dealing in lead, one called Hammond, one called Dalling. Cheeky Charlie must be something to do with both.'

'Lead!' said Jack. 'It's very valuable nowadays, isn't it? I'm always reading about thieves going and stealing it off church roofs. I don't know why churches so often have lead roofs, but they seem to.'

'It looks as if Cheeky Charlie might be going to send a load of lead off somewhere in a truck, and Zeb and the others are going to stop it, and take the lead,' said Peter. 'As you say, it's very valuable, Jack.'

'Charlie must have quite a high position if

he's in both firms,' said Janet. 'Oh, dear – I do wonder what his real name is! Cheeky Charlie! I wonder why they call him that?'

'Because he's bold and has got plenty of cheek, I expect,' said Peter. 'If only Hammond's and Dalling's weren't so far away! We could go and snoop round there and see if we could hear of anyone called Cheeky Charlie.'

'They're miles away,' said Jack, looking at the addresses. 'Well, we've been quite clever, but I don't see that we've got very much farther, really. We just know that Dalling's and Hammond's are firms that deal in lead, which is very valuable stuff, but that's all!'

'Yes. It doesn't take us very far,' said Peter, shutting up the directory. 'We'll have to think a bit harder. Come on, let's go and buy some sweets. Sucking a bit of toffee always seems to help my thinking!'

CHAPTER TWELVE

A game – and a brainwave!

ANOTHER DAY went by, and Saturday came. A
meeting was called for that morning, but nobody had much to say. In fact, it was rather a
dull meeting after the excitement of the last
one. The Seven sat in the shed eating biscuits
provided by Jack's mother, and Scamper was
at the door, on guard as usual.

It was raining outside. The Seven looked out
dismally.

'No good going for a walk, or having a game
of football,' said Peter. 'Let's stay here in the
shed and play a game.'

'Fetch your railway set, Peter,' said Janet.
'And I'll fetch the farm set. We could set out
the lines here in the midst of the toy trees and

farm buildings, looking as if they were real countryside. We've got heaps of farm stuff.'

'Oh yes. Let's do that,' said Pam. 'I love your farm set. It's the nicest and biggest I've ever seen. Do get it! We could set it out, and the boys could put up the railway.'

'It's a jolly good thing to do on a rainy morning like this,' said Jack, pleased. 'I wanted to help Jeff with *his* fine railway the other day, when George came to tea with me, but he was Susie's guest, and she wouldn't have let us join in for anything. You know, she's very suspicious that we're working on something, Peter. She keeps on and on at me to tell her if anything happened at Tigger's Barn that night.'

'Well, just shut her up,' said Peter. 'Scamper, you needn't watch the door any more. You can come and join us, old fellow. The meeting's over.'

Scamper was pleased. He ran round everyone, wagging his tail. Peter fetched his railway set, and Janet and Pam went to get the big farm set. It had absolutely everything, from animals and farm men to trees, fences, troughs and sties!

They all began to put up the two sets – putting together the lines and setting out a proper little countryside, with trees, fences, animals and farm buildings. It really was fun.

Peter suddenly looked up at the window. He had noticed a movement there. He saw a face looking in, and leapt up with such a fierce yell that everyone jumped in alarm.

'It's Jeff,' he cried. 'I wonder if he's snooping round for the Famous Five. After him, Scamper!'

But Jeff had taken to his heels, and, even if Scamper had caught him, nothing would have happened, because the spaniel knew Jeff well and liked him.

'It doesn't really matter Jeff looking in,' said Janet. 'All he'd see would be us having a very peaceful game! Let him stand out in the rain and look in if he wants to!'

The railway lines were ready at last. The three beautiful clockwork engines were attached to their line of trucks. Two were passenger trains and one was a goods train.

'I'll manage one train, you can do another train, Colin, and you can have a third one,

Jack,' said Peter. 'Janet, you do the signals. You're good at those. And, George, you work the points. We mustn't have an accident. You can always switch one of the trains on to another line, if two look like crashing.'

'Right. I'll manage the points,' said George, pleased. 'I like doing those. I love seeing a train being switched off a main-line into a siding.'

The engines were wound up and set going.

They tore round the floor, and George switched them cleverly from one line to another when it seemed there might be an accident.

And, in the middle of all this, Janet suddenly sat up straight, and said in a loud voice: 'WELL, I NEVER!'

The others looked at her.

'What's the matter?' said Peter. 'Well, I never *what*? Why are you looking as if you are going to burst?'

'Points!' said Janet, excitedly. 'Points!' And she waved her hand to where George was sitting working the points, switching the trains from one line to another. 'Oh Peter, don't be so *stupid*! Don't you remember? Those men at Tigger's Barn talked about *points*. Jack said they kept *on* mentioning them. Well, I bet they were *points on some railway line*!'

There was a short silence. Then everyone spoke at once. 'Yes! It could be! Why didn't we think of it before? Of course! Points on the railway!'

The game stopped at once and an eager discussion began.

'Why should they use the points? It must be because they want to switch a train on to another line.'

'Yes, a train that contains something they want to steal – lead, probably!'

'Then it's a goods train. One of the trucks must be carrying the lead they want to steal!'

'The tarpaulin! Would that be covering up the load? Don't you remember? It had to be marked with white at the corner, so that the men would know it.'

'Yes! They wouldn't have to waste time then looking into every truck to see which was the right one. Sometimes there are thirty or forty trucks on a goods train. The white marks on the tarpaulin would tell them at once they had the right truck!'

'Woof,' said Scamper, joining in the general excitement.

Peter turned to him. 'Hey, Scamper, on

guard at the door again, old fellow!' he said, at once. 'The meeting's begun again! On guard!'

Scamper went on guard. The Secret Seven drew close together, suddenly very excited. To think that one simple word had set their brains working like this, and put them on the right track at once!

'You are really clever, Janet,' said Jack, and Janet beamed.

'Oh, anyone might have thought of it,' she said. 'It just rang a bell in my mind somehow, when you kept saying "points". Oh, Peter, where are these points, do you think?'

Peter was following out another idea in his mind. 'I've thought of something else,' he said, his eyes shining. 'Those figures the men kept saying. Six-two, seven-ten. Couldn't they be the times of trains?'

'Oh *yes*! Like when we say Daddy's going to catch the six-twenty home, or the seven-twelve!' cried Pam. 'Six-two – there must be a train that starts somewhere at six-two. Or arrives somewhere then.'

'And they want a foggy or misty, dark night, because then it would be easy to switch the train into some siding,' said Jack. 'A foggy night would be marvellous for them. The engine-driver couldn't possibly see that his train had been switched off on the wrong line. He'd go on till he came to some signal, and the men would be there ready to take the lead from the marked truck – '

'And they'd deal with the surprised engine-driver, and the guard too, I suppose,' said Colin.

There was a silence after this. It suddenly dawned on the Seven that there must be quite a big gang engaged in this particular robbery.

'I think we ought to tell somebody,' said Pam.

Peter shook his head. 'No. Let's find out more if we can. And I'm sure we can now! For instance, let's get a time-table and see if there's a train that arrives anywhere at two minutes past six – 6.2.'

'That's no good,' said Jack, at once. 'Goods trains aren't in the time-tables.'

'Oh no. I forgot that,' said Peter. 'Well, what about one or two of us going down to the station and asking a few questions about goods trains and what time they come in, and where from? We know where the firms of Dalling and Hammond are. Where was it now – Petlington, wasn't it?'

'Yes,' said Janet. 'That's a good idea of yours to go down to the station, Peter. It's stopped raining. Why don't you go now?'

'I will,' said Peter. 'You come with me, Colin. Jack and George have had plenty of excitement so far, but you haven't had very much. Come on down to the station with me.'

So off went the two boys, looking rather thrilled. They really were on the trail now!

Peter and Colin arrived at the station just as a train was coming in. They watched it. Two porters were on the platform, and a man stood with them in dirty blue overalls. He had been working on the line, and had hopped up on to the platform when the train came rumbling in.

The boys waited till the train had gone out. Then they went up to one of the porters.

'Are there any goods trains coming through?' asked Peter. 'We like watching them.'

'There's one in fifteen minutes' time,' said the porter.

'Is it a very long one?' said Colin. 'I once counted forty-seven trucks pulled by a goods engine.'

'The longest one comes in here in the evening,' said the porter. 'How many trucks do you reckon it has as a rule, Zeb?'

The man in dirty overalls rubbed a black hand over his face, and pushed back his cap. 'Well, maybe thirty, maybe forty. It depends.'

The boys looked at one another. *Zeb!* The porter had called the linesman *Zeb!* Could it be – could it *possibly* be the same Zeb that had met the other two men at Tigger's Barn?

They looked at him. He wasn't much to look at, certainly, a thin, mean-faced little man, very dirty, and with hair much too long. Zeb! It was such an unusual name that the boys felt sure they must be face to face with the Zeb who had been up at the old tumbledown house.

'Er – what time does this goods train come in the evening?' asked Peter, finding his tongue again at last.

'It comes in about six o'clock twice a week,' said Zeb. 'Six-two, it's supposed to be here, but sometimes it's late.'

'Where does it come from?' asked Colin.

'Plenty of places!' said Zeb, 'Turleigh, Idlesston, Hayley, Garton, Petlington . . .'

'Petlington!' said Colin, before he could stop himself. That was the place where the firms of Dalling and Hammond were. Peter scowled at him, and Colin hurried to cover up his mistake in calling attention to the town they were so interested in.

'Petlington, yes, go on, where else?' said Colin.

The linesman gave him another string of names, and the boys listened. But they had learnt already a good deal of what they wanted to know.

The 6.2 was a goods train, that came in twice a week, and Petlington was one of the places it came from, probably with a truck or two added there, full of lead goods from Hammond's and Dalling's! Lead pipes? Sheets of lead? The boys had no idea, and it didn't really matter. It was lead, anyway, valuable lead, they were sure of that! Lead sent off by Cheeky Charlie for his firms.

'We've been playing with my model railway this morning,' said Peter, suddenly thinking of a way to ask about points and switches. 'It's a fine one, it's got points to switch my trains from one line to another. Very good they are too, as good as real points!'

'Ah, you want to ask my mate about *them*,' said Zeb. 'He's got plenty to deal with. He uses them to switch the goods trains from one part

of the line to another. They often have to go into sidings, you know.'

'Does he switch the 6.2 into a siding?' said Peter. 'Or does it go straight through on the main-line?'

'Straight through,' said Zeb. 'No, Larry only switches the goods trains that have to be unloaded near here. The 6.2 goes right on to Swindon. You'll see it this evening if you come down.'

Peter had given a quick look at Colin to see if he had noticed the name of Zeb's mate – Larry! Zeb and Larry – what an enormous piece of luck! Colin gave a quick wink at Peter. Yes, he had noticed all right! He began to look excited.

'I wish we could see Larry working the points,' said Peter. 'It must be fun. I expect the switches are quite different from the ones on my railway lines at home.'

Zeb laughed. 'You bet they are! Ours take some moving! Look, would you like to walk along the line with me, and I'll show you some switches that send a train off into a siding? It's about a mile up the line.'

Peter took a look at his watch. He would be very late for his dinner, but this was really important. Why, he might see the very points that Larry was going to use one dark, foggy night!

'Look out the kids don't get knocked down by a train,' the porter warned Zeb, as the linesman took the two boys down on to the track with him.

The boys looked at him with scorn. As if they couldn't tell when a train was coming!

It seemed a very long way up the line. Zeb had a job of work not far from the points. He left his tools by the side of the line he was to repair, and took the boys to where a number of lines crossed one another. He explained how the points worked.

'You pull this lever for that line, see? Watch how the rails move so that they lead to that other line over there, instead of letting the train keep on this line.'

Colin and Peter did a little pulling of levers themselves, and they found it exceptionally hard work.

'Does the 6.2 come on this line?' asked Peter, innocently.

'Yes. But it goes straight on; it doesn't get switched to one side,' said Zeb. 'It never has goods for this district; it goes on to Swindon. Now don't you ever mess about on the railway by yourselves, or the police will be after you straight away!'

'We won't,' promised the two boys.

'Well, I must get on with my job,' said Zeb, not sounding as if he wanted to at all. 'So long! Hope I've told you what you wanted to know.'

He certainly had, much, much more than he imagined. Colin and Peter could hardly believe their luck. They made their way to the side of the line, and stood there for a while.

'We ought really to go and explore the siding,' said Peter. 'But we're dreadfully late. Bother! We forgot to ask what evenings the goods train comes in from Petlington!'

'Let's get back, and come again this afternoon,' said Colin. 'I'm so hungry. We can find out the two days the goods train comes through when we're here this afternoon, and explore the siding too.'

They left the railway and went to the road. They were both so excited that they could hardly stop talking. 'Fancy bumping into Zeb! Zeb himself! And hearing about Larry in charge of the points! Why, everything's as plain as can be. What a good thing Janet had the brain-wave this morning about points! My goodness, we are in luck!'

'We'll be back this afternoon as soon as we can,' said Peter. 'I vote the whole lot of us go. Gosh, this *is* getting exciting!'

CHAPTER THIRTEEN

An exciting afternoon

BOTH PETER'S mother and Colin's were very angry when they arrived back so late for their dinner. Janet was so full of curiosity to know what had happened that she could hardly wait till Peter had finished. He kept frowning at her as he gobbled down his hot stew, afraid that she would ask some awkward questions.

He sent her round to collect the Secret Seven, and they all arrived in a very short time, though Colin was late because he had to finish his dinner.

Peter told them everything, and they listened, thrilled. Well, what a tale! To meet Zeb like that, and to have him telling them so much that they wanted to know!

'Little did he know why we asked him so many questions!' said Colin, with a grin. 'I must say he was quite nice to us, though he's a mean-looking man with shifty eyes.'

'This afternoon we will all go to the siding,' said Peter. 'We'll find out what days that goods train comes along, too.'

So off they went. First they went to the station and found the porter again. He had nothing much to do and was pleased to talk to them. He told them tales of this, that and the other on the railway, and gradually Peter guided him to the subject of goods trains.

'Here comes one,' said the porter. 'It won't stop at the station, though – no passengers to get on or off, you see. Want to count the trucks? It's not a very long train.'

Most of the trucks were open ones, and they carried all kinds of things, coal, bricks, machinery, crates. The train rumbled by slowly, and the Seven counted thirty-two trucks.

'I'd rather like to see that goods train Zeb told us about,' said Peter to the porter. 'The one that comes from Petlington and beyond,

the 6.2, I think he said. It's sometimes a very long one, isn't it?'

'Yes. Well, you'd have to come on Tuesday or Friday,' said the porter. 'But it's dark then, so you won't see much. Look, the guard of that last goods train is waving to you!'

They waved back. The goods train got smaller and smaller in the distance and at last disappeared.

'I wonder things aren't stolen out of those open trucks,' said Peter, innocently.

'Oh, they are,' said the porter. 'There's been a whole lot of stealing lately, yes, even a car taken out of one truck, though you mightn't believe it! Some gang at work, they say. Beats me how they do it! Well, you kids, I must go and do a spot of work. So long!'

The Seven wandered off. They walked by the side of the track for about a mile until they came to where the points were that Zeb had explained that morning.

Peter pointed them out. 'That's where they plan to switch the goods train off to a side-line,' he said. 'I wish we knew which evening. I think it must be soon, though, because that note

George got said that everything was ready and going O.K.'

They followed the side-line, walking by the side of the railway. The line meandered off all by itself and finally came into a little goods yard, which seemed to be completely deserted at that moment.

Big gates led into the goods yard. They were open to let in lorries that came to take the goods unloaded from trucks sent down the side-line. But only empty trucks stood on the little line now, and not a soul was about. It was plain that no goods train was expected for some time.

'This is a very lonely little place,' said Colin. 'If a goods train was diverted down here, nobody would hear it or see it, except those who would be waiting for it! I bet there will be a lorry creeping in here some evening, ready to take the lead sheets or pipes or whatever they are, from the truck whose tarpaulin is marked with white lines!'

'What about coming here on Tuesday evening, just in *case* that's the night they've arranged?' said Jack, suddenly. 'Then, if we saw anything happening, we could telephone the police. And before Zeb and Larry and the other two could finish their unloading we could get the police here. I say, wouldn't that be a thrill?'

'I don't know. I think really we ought to get in touch with that big Inspector we like,' said Peter. 'We know quite enough now to be sure of what we say. The only thing we *don't* know is whether it's this Tuesday or if it's to be later on.'

They stood together, arguing, and nobody saw a burly policeman sauntering in through the open gates. He stared when he saw the children, and stood watching them.

'I'd like to see those points,' said Colin, getting tired of the argument. 'Show me them, Peter. We'll look out for trains.'

Peter forgot that children were not allowed to trespass on the railway lines. He set off up the side-line with the others, walking in the middle of the lines on his way to the points.

A loud voice hailed them. 'Hey, you kids there! What do you think you're doing, trespassing like that? You come back here. I've got something to say to you.'

'Let's run!' said Pam, in a panic. 'Don't let him catch us.'

'No. We can't run,' said Peter. 'I forgot we ought not to walk on the lines like this. Come back and explain, and if we say we're sorry, we'll be all right!'

So he led all the Seven back into the goods yard. The policeman came up to them, frowning.

'Now you look here,' he said; 'there's been

too much nonsense from children on the railways lately. I've a good mind to take all your names and addresses and make a complaint to your parents about you.'

'But we weren't doing a thing!' said Peter, indignantly. 'We're sorry we trespassed, but honestly we weren't doing a scrap of harm.'

'What are you doing in this here goods yard?' said the policeman. 'Up to some mischief, no doubt!'

'We're not,' said Peter.

'Well, what did you come here for, then,' said the policeman. 'Go on, tell me. You didn't come here for nothing.'

'Tell him,' said Barbara, frightened and almost crying.

The policeman became very suspicious at once when he heard that there was something to tell. 'Oho! So there *was* something you were after!' he said. 'Now you just tell me, or I'll take your names and addresses!'

Peter wasn't going to tell this bad-tempered man anything. For one thing, he wouldn't believe the extraordinary tale that the Secret Seven had to tell, and for another, Peter wasn't going to give all his secrets away! No, if he was going to tell anyone, he would tell his father, or the Inspector they all liked so much!

It ended in the big policeman losing his temper thoroughly and taking down all their names and addresses, one by one. It was really maddening. To think they had come there to help to catch a gang of clever thieves, and had had their names taken for trespassing!

'I'll get told off if my father hears about this,'

said Colin, dolefully. 'Oh, Peter, let's tell our nice Inspector everything, before that policeman goes round to our parents.'

But Peter was angry and obstinate. 'No!' he said. 'We'll settle this affair ourselves, and the police can come in at the last moment, when we've done everything, yes, that horrid man, too, who took our names. Think of his face if he has to come along to this goods yard one night to catch thieves *we've* tracked down, instead of him! I'll feel jolly pleased to crow over him!'

'I'd like to come, too, on that night,' said Janet.

'Well I think just a few of us should go. If things turn dangerous it'll be better if there's just four of us rather than seven!'

No one could argue with that, so they decided that Jack, Colin, George and Peter should go alone.

CHAPTER FOURTEEN

Tuesday evening at last!

THERE WAS a meeting the next morning to talk over everything and to make arrangements for Tuesday. It was a proper November day, and a mist hung everywhere.

'My father says there will be a fog before tomorrow,' announced Peter. 'If so those men are going to be lucky on Tuesday. I don't expect the driver of the engine will even guess his train's on the side-line when the points send him there! He won't be able to see a thing.'

'I wish Tuesday would buck up and come,' said Jack. 'Susie *knows* there's something up, and she and her Famous Five are just *longing* to know what it is! Won't she be wild when she knows that it was her silly trick that put us on to all this?'

'Yes. I guess that will be the end of the Famous Five,' said Colin. 'Hey, Peter, look here. I managed to get hold of a railway map. My father had one. It shows the lines from Petlington, and all the points and everything. Jack, do you think it could have been a map like this that Zeb and Larry and the other man were looking at in Tigger's Barn?'

'Yes. It may have been,' said Jack. 'I bet those men have played this kind of game before. They know the railway so well. Oh, I do wish Tuesday would come!'

Tuesday did come at last. Not one of the Secret Seven could do good work at school that day. They kept on and on thinking of the coming night. Peter looked out of the window a hundred times that morning!

'Dad was right,' he thought. 'The fog did come down, a real November fog. And tonight it will be so thick that there will be fog-signals on the railways. We shall hear them go off.'

The four boys had arranged to meet after tea, with Scamper. Peter thought it would be a good thing to take him with them in case anything went wrong.

They all had torches. Peter felt to see if he had any sweets in his pocket to share with his friends. He had! Jolly good! He shivered with excitement.

He nearly didn't go with the others, because

his mother saw him putting his coat on, and was horrified to think that he was going out into the fog.

'You'll get lost,' she said. 'You mustn't go.'

'I'm meeting the others,' said Peter, desperately. 'I *must* go, Mummy.'

'I really can't let you,' said his mother. 'Well – not unless you take Scamper with you. He'll know the way home if you don't!'

'Oh, I'm taking Scamper, of *course*,' said Peter thankfully, and escaped at once, Scamper at his heels. He met the others at his gate and they set off.

The thick fog swirled round them, and their torches could hardly pierce it. Then they heard the bang-bang of the fog-signals on the rail-way.

'I bet Zeb and the rest are pleased with this fog!' said Colin. 'Look, there's the fence that runs beside the railway. If we keep close to that we can't lose our way.'

They arrived at the goods yard about five minutes to six, and went cautiously in at the gates, which were open. All the boys had rubber-soled shoes on, and they carefully switched off their torches as they went quietly into the goods yard.

They heard the sound of a lorry's engine throbbing, and stopped. Voices came to them, low voices, and then they saw a lantern held by someone.

'The gang are here, and the lorry sent by Cheeky Charlie!' whispered Jack. 'You can just see it over there. I bet it's got the name of Hammond or Dalling on it!'

'It *was* this Tuesday,' said Colin, in relief. 'I did hope we hadn't come all the way here in this fog for nothing.'

Bang! Bang-bang!

More fog-signals went off and yet more. The boys knew when trains were running over the main-line some distance away because of the sudden explosions of the fog-signals, warning the drivers to look out for the real signals or to go slowly.

'What's the time?' whispered George.

'It's about half-past six now,' whispered back Peter. 'The 6.2 is late because of the fog. It may be along any time now, or it may be very late, of course.'

Bᴀɴɢ! Another fog-signal went off in the next few minutes. The boys wondered if it had gone off under the wheels of the late goods train.

It had. The driver put his head out of his train and looked for the signal. It shone green.

He could go on. He went on slowly, not knowing he was on the wrong line! Larry was there at the points, well-hidden by the darkness and the fog, and he had switched the goods train carefully on to the little side-line!

The goods train left the main-line. It would not go through the station tonight, it would only go into the little goods yard, where silent men awaited it. Larry switched the levers again, so that the next train would go safely on to the main-line. He did not want half a dozen trains on the side-line together! Then he ran down the single-line after the slow-moving train.

'It's coming! I can hear it,' whispered Peter suddenly, and he caught hold of Jack's arm. 'Let's go over there by that shed. We can see everything without being seen. Come on!'

Rumble-rumble-rumble! The goods train came nearer. The red eye of a lamp gleamed in the fog. Now what was going to happen?

CHAPTER FIFTEEN

In the goods yard

A foG-SIGNAL went off just where the gang wanted the train to stop. Bang!

The engine pulled up at once, and the trucks behind clang-clanged as they bumped into one another. A hurried talk had gone on between Zeb, Larry and four other men by the coach. The boys could hear every word.

'We'll tell him he's on the wrong line. We'll pretend to be surprised to see him there. Larry, you tell him he'd better stay on this side-line till the fog clears and he can get orders and go back. Take him off to that shed and hot up some tea or something. Keep him there while we do the job!'

The others nodded.

Peter whispered to Jack: 'They're going to tell the engine-driver that he's run off the main-line by mistake into this side-line, and then take him off out of the way, the guard too, I expect. There won't be any fighting, which is a good thing.'

'Sh!' said Jack. 'Look, the engine-driver is jumping down. He's lost, I expect! Doesn't know where he is!'

'Hey, there, engine-driver, you're on the side-line!' called Larry's voice, and he ran up to the engine, a lamp swaying in his hands. 'You ought to be on the main-line, running through the station.'

'Ay, I should be,' said the driver, puzzled. 'There must have been some mistake at the points. Am I safe here, mate?'

'Safe as can be!' called back Larry, cheerily. 'Don't you worry! You're in a goods yard, well out of the way of main-line traffic. Better not move till you get orders, this fog's terrible!'

'Good thing I got on to a side-line, that's all I can say,' said the driver. The guard came up at that moment from the last van, and joined in the conversation. He thought it peculiar.

'Someone making a mess of the points,' he grumbled. 'Now we'll be here for the night, and my missus is expecting me for supper.'

'Well, you may be home for breakfast if the fog clears,' said the driver, comfortingly.

The guard didn't think so. He was very gloomy.

'Well, mates, come along to this shed,' said Larry. 'There's an oil-stove there, and we'll light up and have a cup of something hot. Don't worry about telephoning for orders. I'll do all that.'

'Who are you?' asked the gloomy guard.

'Who, me? I'm in charge of this yard,' said Larry, most untruthfully. 'Don't you worry now. It's a blessing you got on to this side-line. I bet your orders will be to stay here for the night. I'll have to find somewhere for you to settle down.'

They all disappeared into the shed. A glow soon came from the window. Peter daringly peeped in, and saw the three men round an oil stove, and a kettle on top to boil water for tea.

Then things moved remarkably quickly. Zeb disappeared down the side-line to look for the truck covered by the tarpaulin with white marks. It was the seventh one, as he informed the others when he came back.

'We'll start up the lorry, and take it to the truck,' he said. 'Fortunately it's just where the yard begins, so we shan't have to carry the stuff far. Good thing, too, because it's heavy.'

The lorry was started up, and ran cautiously up the yard to the far end. There it stopped, presumably by the seventh truck. The four boys went silently through the fog and watched what happened for a minute or two.

The men were untying the tarpaulin by the light of a railway lantern. Soon it was entirely off. Jack could see the white paint at one corner that had marked it for the men.

Then began a pulling and tugging and painting as the men hauled up the goods inside. What were they? The boys couldn't see.

'Sheets of lead, I think,' whispered Colin. 'Peter, when are we going to telephone the police? Don't you think we'd better do that now?'

'Yes,' whispered back Peter. 'Come on.

There's a telephone in that little brick building over there. I noticed telephone wires going to the chimney there this afternoon. One of the windows is a bit open. We'll get in there. Where's Scamper? Oh, there you are. Now, not a sound, old boy!'

Scamper had behaved perfectly. Not a bark, not a whine had come from him, though he was very puzzled by the evening's happenings. He trotted at Peter's heels as the four boys went to telephone.

They had to pass the lorry on the way. Peter stopped dead and listened. No one was in the lorry. The men were still unloading the truck.

To the astonishment of the other three, he left them, leapt up into the driving seat and down again.

'Whatever are you doing?' whispered Jack.

'I took the key that turns on the engine!' said Peter, excited. 'Now they can't drive the lorry away!'

'Gosh!' said the others, lost in admiration at Peter's quickness. 'You *are* smart, Peter!'

They went to the little stone building. The

door was locked, but, as Peter said, a window was open just a little. It was easy to force it up. In went Peter and flashed his torch round quickly to find the telephone. Ah yes, there it was. Good!

He switched off his torch and picked up the receiver. He heard the operator's voice.

'Number, please?'

'Police station – quickly!' said Peter.

And in two seconds a voice came again. 'Police station here.'

'Is the Inspector there, please?' asked Peter, urgently. 'Please tell him it's Peter, and I want to speak to him quickly.'

This peculiar message was passed on to the Inspector, who happened to be in the room. He came to the telephone at once.

'Yes, yes? Peter who? Oh *you*, Peter! What's up?'

Peter told him. 'Sir, I can't tell you all the details now, but the 6.2 goods train has been switched off the main-line on to the side-line here, near Kepley, where there's a goods yard. And there is a gang of men unloading lead from one of the waggons into a lorry nearby. I think a man called Cheeky Charlie is in charge of things, sir.'

'Cheeky Charlie! Chee – How do *you* know anything about that fellow?' cried the Inspector, filled with amazement. 'All right, don't waste time telling me now. I'll send men out straight away. Look out for them, and look out for yourselves too. That gang is dangerous. Cheeky Charlie, well, my word!'

CHAPTER SIXTEEN

Hurrah for the Secret Seven!

IT SEEMED a long time before any police cars came. The four boys were so excited that they could not keep still. Peter felt as if he really must go and see how the gang was getting on.

He crept out into the yard, and made his way to the lorry. It was dark there, and quiet. He crept forward, and suddenly bumped into someone standing still beside it.

The someone gave a shout and caught him. 'Here, who's this? What are you doing?'

Then a light was flashed on him, and Zeb's voice said: 'You! The kid who was asking questions the other day! What are you up to?'

He shook Peter so roughly that the boy

almost fell over. And then Scamper came flying up!

'Grrrrrrrr!' He flew at Zeb and nipped him sharply on the leg. Zeb gave a yell. Two of the other men came running up. 'What's the matter? What's up?'

'A boy – and a dog!' growled Zeb. 'We'd better get going. Is the unloading finished? That kid may give the alarm.'

'Where is he? Why didn't you hang on to him?' said one of the men, angrily.

'The dog bit me, and I had to let the boy go,' said Zeb, rubbing his leg. 'They've both disappeared into the fog. Come on, hurry, I've got the wind up now.'

Peter had shot back to the others, alarmed at being so nearly caught. He bent down and fondled Scamper. 'Good boy!' he whispered. 'Brave dog! Well done, Scamper!'

Scamper wagged his tail, pleased. He didn't understand in the least why Peter should have brought him to this peculiar place in a thick fog, but he was quite happy to be with him anywhere.

'When's that police car coming?' whispered

Colin, shivering as much with excitement as with cold.

'Soon, I expect,' whispered back Peter. 'Ah, here it comes – no, two of them!'

The sound of cars coming down the road that led to the goods yards was plainly to be heard. They came slowly, because of the fog. They would have got there very much more quickly if the evening had been clear.

They came into the yard and stopped. Peter ran to the first one. It was driven by the Inspector, and had four policemen in it.

The second car was close behind, and police-men in plain clothes tumbled swiftly out of it.

'Sir! You've come just in time!' said Peter. 'Their lorry is over there. They've loaded it now. You'll catch them just at the right mo-ment!'

The police ran over to the dark shape in the fog, the big lorry. Zeb, Larry, Cheeky Charlie and the other men were all in it, with the load of lead behind, but try as Zeb would he could not find the starting-key of the lorry!

'Start her up quickly, you ninny!' said Cheeky Charlie. 'The police are here! Drive the lorry at them if they try to stop us!'

'The key's gone. It must have dropped down,' wailed Zeb, and flashed a torch on to the floor below the steering-wheel. But it was not a bit of good looking there, of course. It was safely in Peter's pocket!

The police closed round the silent lorry. 'Game's up, Charlie,' said the Inspector's stern voice. 'You coming quietly, or not? We've got you right on the spot!'

'You wouldn't have, if we could have got this lorry to move!' shouted Zeb, angrily. 'Who's got the key? That's what I want to know. Who's got it?'

'I have,' called Peter. 'I took it out myself so that you couldn't get away in the lorry!'

'Good boy! Smart lad!' said a nearby police-man, admiringly, and gave the delighted Peter a thump on the back.

The fog suddenly thinned, and the scene became clearer in the light of many torches and lamps. The engine-driver and the guard came out of the shed in amazement, wondering what was happening. They had been left comfortably there by Zeb, drinking tea and playing cards.

The gang made no fuss. It wasn't worth it, with so many strong men around! They were bundled into the police cars, which drove away at a faster speed than they had come, thanks to the thinning of the fog!

'I'll walk back with you,' said the Inspector's cheerful voice. 'There's no room in the cars for me now. There's a bit of a squash there at the moment!'

He told the engine-driver to report what had happened to his headquarters by telephone, and left the astonished man, and the equally astonished fireman and guard, to look after themselves and their train.

Then he and the four boys trudged back to Peter's house. How amazed his mother was when she opened the door and found four of them with the big Inspector!

'Oh dear, what have they been up to now?' she said. 'A policeman has just been round complaining about Peter trespassing on the railway the other day, with his friends. Oh, don't say he's done anything terribly wrong!'

'Well, he's certainly been trespassing on the railway again,' said the Inspector, with a broad smile, 'but what he's done this time is terribly right, not terribly wrong. Let me come in and tell you.'

So, with a very excited Janet listening, the tale of that evening was told.

'And, you see,' finished the Inspector, 'we've got our hands on Cheeky Charlie at last. He's the boss of this gang that robs the goods trucks all over the place. A clever fellow but not *quite* so clever as the Secret Seven!'

The Inspector left at last, beaming, full of admiration once more for the Secret Seven. Peter turned to the others.

'Tomorrow,' he said solemnly, but with his face glowing – 'tomorrow we call a meeting of the Secret Seven – and we ask the Famous Five to come along too!'

'But why?' said Janet, surprised.

'Just so that we can tell them how the Secret Seven manage their affairs!' said Peter. 'And to thank them for putting us on the track of this most exciting adventure!'

'Ha! Susie won't like that!' said Jack.

'She certainly won't,' said Janet. 'Famous Five indeed! This will be the end of *them*!'

'Up with the Secret Seven!' said Jack, grinning. 'Hurrah for us – hip-hip-hurrah!'